A Note to Parents and Caregivers:

Read-it! Readers are for children who are just starting on the amazing road to reading. These beautiful books support both the acquisition of reading skills and the love of books.

The RED LEVEL presents familiar topics using common words and repeating sentence patterns.

The BLUE LEVEL presents new ideas using a larger vocabulary and varied sentence structure.

The YELLOW LEVEL presents more challenging ideas, a broad vocabulary, and wide variety in sentence structure.

The GREEN LEVEL presents more complex ideas, an extended vocabulary range, and expanded language structures.

When sharing a book with your child, read in short stretches, pausing often to talk about the pictures. Have your child turn the pages and point to the pictures and familiar words. Be sure to reread favorite stories or parts of stories.

There is no right or wrong way to share books with children. Find time to read with your child, and pass on the legacy of literacy.

Adria F. Klein, Ph.D.
Professor Emeritus
California State University
San Bernardino, California

Managing Editor: Bob Temple
Creative Director: Terri Foley
Editor: Peggy Henrikson
Editorial Adviser: Andrea Cascardi
Copy Editor: Laurie Kahn
Designer: Nathan Gassman
Page production: Picture Window Books
The illustrations in this book were rendered with watercolor.

Picture Window Books
5115 Excelsior Boulevard
Suite 232
Minneapolis, MN 55416
1-877-845-8392
www.picturewindowbooks.com

Library of Congress Cataloging-in-Publication Data
Blackaby, Susan.
Thumbelina / by Hans Christian Andersen ; adapted by
Susan Blackaby ; illustrated by Charlene DeLage.
p. cm. — (Read-it! readers fairy tales)
Summary: After being kidnapped by a toad, a beautiful girl
no bigger than a thumb has many adventures and makes many
animal friends before meeting the perfect mate just her size.
ISBN 1-4048-0225-8
[1. Fairy tales.] I. DeLage, Charlene, 1944– ill. II. Andersen, H. C.
(Hans Christian), 1805–1875. Tommelise. English. III. Title. IV. Series.
PZ8.B5595 Th 2004
[E]—dc21
                                    2003006112

Thumbelina

by Hans Christian Andersen

Adapted by Susan Blackaby
Illustrated by Charlene DeLage

Special thanks to our advisers for their expertise:
Adria F. Klein, Ph.D.
Professor Emeritus, California State University
San Bernardino, California

Kathy Baxter, M.A.
Former Coordinator of Children's Services
Anoka County (Minnesota) Library

Susan Kesselring, M.A.
Literacy Educator
Rosemount-Apple Valley-Eagan (Minnesota) School District

PICTURE WINDOW BOOKS
Minneapolis, Minnesota

There once was a woman who didn't have any children. She went to a fairy for help. "How can I get a little child?" she asked.

"Plant this seed in a pot. See what happens!" said the fairy.
The woman did as she was told.
The seed grew into a tulip.

Inside the tulip sat a girl as tiny
as a thumb. The woman named her
Thumbelina. The child was so small
she could sleep in a walnut shell
with a rose-petal blanket.

Thumbelina had a perfect life.

Then one night a toad came by.

"You'll make a fine wife for my son!

You're coming with me!" Toad said.

Toad took Thumbelina to the swamp and set her on a lily pad. "Meet your husband!" croaked Toad. Toad's slimy son said, *"Ribbit!"*

"No! No! No!" cried Thumbelina.
Fish heard her and nibbled at the
lily's roots until the pad broke free.
Thumbelina floated away.

As Thumbelina swirled along,
a beetle grabbed her and flew up
into his tree house. Beetle showed
her to his friend.

"Isn't she a pretty little thing?"
"Pretty ugly, you mean," said
Beetle's friend. "Look! She has
only two legs and no feelers at all!"

Beetle decided that he did not like Thumbelina after all. He dropped her on top of a daisy and flew away.

Thumbelina spent her lonely summer under a leaf. Then winter came, and it began to snow. Thumbelina had to find a home.

Thumbelina found a little den.
It belonged to a field mouse.
"You poor thing! Come inside!"
said Mouse. She liked Thumbelina
at once.

"Stay with me for the winter," said Mouse. "All you have to do is clean the house and tell me stories."

Thumbelina and Mouse were a
cozy pair. One day Mouse said,
"A neighbor is coming to see us.
He'd be a good husband for you."

Thumbelina met the neighbor,
a gloomy mole in a black velvet coat.
Thumbelina was polite, but she
did not like him very much.

A tunnel ran between Mouse's den and Mole's hole. In it lay a bird that was frozen stiff. Mole and Mouse did not care at all.

"Silly tweeter didn't have a bit of sense," said Mole. Thumbelina felt sorry for Bird. When no one was looking, she gave Bird a kiss.

That night, Thumbelina took a warm
blanket to Bird. She gave him a hug.
Thump! Thump! Bird's heart
was beating!

Bird wasn't dead. He was just cold. Thumbelina cared for him until he was strong enough to fly.

"Come away with me," said Bird.

Thumbelina said, "I can't leave
Mouse. She's been good to me."
Bird flew into the sunshine, and
Thumbelina waved good-bye.

In the den, Mouse was in a tizzy.
"Mole has decided to marry lucky
little teeny-tiny you!" she said.
"We have 100 things to do!"

"I can't marry that old fur ball
and live in a dark hole!" cried
Thumbelina. "I just can't!"
"Count your blessings," said Mouse.

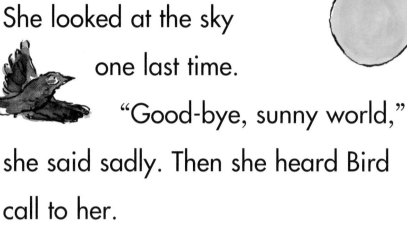

Thumbelina went outside.
She looked at the sky
one last time.
"Good-bye, sunny world,"
she said sadly. Then she heard Bird
call to her.

"Tweet! Hop on!" he said.
"We'll fly far away from doomy,
gloomy Mole!" So they flew south
until they came to a castle by a lake.

Bird set Thumbelina down beside a yellow flower. Inside the flower was a prince. He took one look at Thumbelina and fell in love.

"Say you'll be my wife!" said the prince. Thumbelina thought of slimy Toad and gloomy Mole. "Yes! Yes! Yes!" she said happily.

All the flowers opened, and the flower fairies greeted Thumbelina. They gave her silver wings and named her Maia.

Bird sang at the wedding, but he was sad. He, too, loved Maia. In the spring, Bird bid her farewell. He flew north, telling this story to all who would listen.

Levels for *Read-it!* Readers

Blue Level

Little Red Riding Hood, by Maggie Moore 1-4048-0064-6
The Goose that Laid the Golden Egg, by Mark White 1-4048-0219-3
The Three Little Pigs, by Maggie Moore 1-4048-0071-9

Yellow Level

Cinderella, by Barrie Wade 1-4048-0052-2
Goldilocks and the Three Bears, by Barrie Wade 1-4048-0057-3
Jack and the Beanstalk, by Maggie Moore 1-4048-0059-X
The Ant and the Grasshopper, by Mark White 1-4048-0217-7
The Fox and the Grapes, by Mark White 1-4048-0218-5
The Three Billy Goats Gruff, by Barrie Wade 1-4048-0070-0
The Tortoise and the Hare, by Mark White 1-4048-0215-0
The Wolf in Sheep's Clothing, by Mark White 1-4048-0220-7

Green Level

The Emperor's New Clothes, adapted by Susan Blackaby 1-4048-0224-X
The Lion and the Mouse, by Mark White 1-4048-0216-9
The Little Mermaid, adapted by Susan Blackaby 1-4048-0221-5
The Princess and the Pea, adapted by Susan Blackaby 1-4048-0223-1
The Steadfast Tin Soldier, adapted by Susan Blackaby 1-4048-0226-6
The Ugly Duckling, adapted by Susan Blackaby 1-4048-0222-3
Thumbelina, adapted by Susan Blackaby 1-4048-0225-8